GRANDMA'S STORIES

Volume 15

Tales of the Wild West Series

Rick Steber

Illustrations by Don Gray

NOTE
GRANDMA'S STORIES is the fifteenth book in the
Tales of the Wild West series.

GRANDMA'S STORIES
Volume 15
Tales of the Wild West series

All rights reserved.
Copyright © 1990 by Rick Steber
Illustrations Copyright © 1990 by Don Gray
ISBN 0-945134-09-6

The book may not be reproduced in whole or in
part, nor utilized in any form or by any means,
without written permission from the copyright
owner. Printed in the West.

Bonanza Publishing
Box 204
Prineville, Oregon 97754

Tales of the Wild West

INTRODUCTION

The Grandma I remember was old. But in her younger days she had come west with Grandpa. Working together they built a house in the wilderness. It was Grandma who made that house into a home.

While Grandpa was working in the fields it fell to Grandma to raise the children. And she was the one who cleaned, cooked, baked, washed and sewed. She tended the chickens, milked the cows and churned the cream to butter. When necessity arose, like the time a horse rolled on Grandpa and he was laid up for nearly a year, Grandma demonstrated she could take on a man's work as well as her own.

Grandma's preferred domain was her kitchen. It was a room dominated by the cheery warmth of a wood stove and the sweet aroma of baking pies. While Grandma worked, frequently pausing to wipe her calloused hands on her freshly ironed white apron, she talked—telling stories of pioneering days, tales handed down and interesting things that had happened to family members, friends and neighbors.

My children will know their great-grandmother because of the stories I will share with them, and from the words Grandma carefully wrote in her journal. Every evening, no matter how trying her day had been, she always took a few moments to reflect and describe things from the day that were important to her—a laughing child chasing a butterfly across the pasture, the lovely fragrance of wildflowers in bloom, the beauty of a field of wheat dancing in an afternoon breeze.... When Grandma finished the entries she would close her journal, blow out the candle flame and say aloud, "And so ends another glorious day."

THE CURE

In the early days of the westward migration, mothers and grandmothers were protectors of the health and welfare of their families. They were responsible for doctoring every illness that came along—measles, mumps, fevers and diarrhea. They coped with severe sunburn, alkali poisoning, rattlesnake bites, broken bones and occasionally injuries from gunshot wounds and Indian arrows.

Most pioneer women had a wealth of folk wisdom and natural remedies that had been handed down to them. They knew that a paste of vinegar and salt repelled mosquitoes. Gunpowder dissolved warts. Liniments were made from goose grease, skunk oil or rendered animal fat. Medicinal teas were brewed from sunflower seeds, chamomile and yarrow. Bee bites and snake bites were treated with a compress of raw chicken meat, a splash of whiskey or a slug of chewing tobacco. A wedge of well-salted pork soothed an earache. Whiskey and honey cured a bad cough. Some women claimed turpentine would cure most any ailment and liberally used it on open cuts and infections, in compresses, and even laced it with sugar and administered it orally to cure sore throats.

Indian remedies incorporating roots, barks, berries, tonics and powders were used to alleviate the symptoms of many illnesses and injuries. But more often than not, the first and only medicine administered was warm broth, plenty of rest and a liberal dose of motherly love.

RETURNING HOME

In 1927 the Christiansen family, which included two children, departed from Indiana to start a new life out west. They drove a Reo club coupe and pulled a homemade trailer piled high with everything they owned, including the family dog, Midgie.

Along the way they ran out of money and were forced to sell their car, trailer and belongings. On Christmas Eve they found themselves in Reno, Nevada, destitute and homeless. The Red Cross provided the family with a free night's lodging and a turkey dinner with all the trimmings on Christmas Day.

Work was hard to come by in Reno. Dozens of men lined up for every job that came open and the Christiansens decided their only recourse, if they were to survive, was to try to hitchhike back to Indiana. A good Samaritan warned them, "This is the dead of winter. You can't hitchhike with those little children. If you get stranded, they'll freeze to death." He arranged for the Salvation Army to provide the family with train tickets.

But a problem arose—the Salvation Army refused to pay for the dog's passage. The children cried when it was suggested Midgie be left behind. A determined Mrs. Christiansen marched across the street to a pawn shop and hocked her wedding ring to buy a ticket for Midgie.

An hour before the train was scheduled to depart, Midgie gave birth to one puppy, then two, three, four and on until there were nine. When Mr. Christiansen handed the box of squirming puppies to the freight master the man looked at the single ticket, shook his head, and never said a word concerning the additional passengers. He simply loaded the box in the freight car and the Christiansen family, along with Midgie and her pups, returned to Indiana.

3

WOMEN'S CAMP

During the days of the Great Depression Sarah Wertz worked as an agent for the federally-subsidized Home Demonstration Program. She traveled to rural areas promoting canning and sewing and giving tips on home decorating and practical landscaping.

After every class women thanked Sarah, often saying this had been the first time in months they had had the opportunity to get out of the house, spend time with other women and actually indulge themselves in learning something new. Their excitement was infectious and eventually Sarah proposed to one group, "What would you think about having a retreat for women, a permanent place where we could get together, socialize and learn? No children or husbands allowed. One week a year our families can fend for themselves. Maybe they will learn to appreciate all we do for them."

The women were wildly enthusiastic and before long Camp Wywona had been established on the Umpqua River south of Roseburg, Oregon. It proved to be a popular place for women to gather. Sarah led long walks in the woods and taught the ladies about birds and wildlife and which plants were safe to eat. Around the campfire the women entertained themselves with skits and sing-alongs. And for fun they swam in a private swimming hole.

One morning a group of women decided to go for a swim and discovered a body floating in the water. The sheriff was called and he found a small log dressed up with pants and a shirt to look like a body. He learned the hoax was nothing more than a practical joke several of the lonely husbands had played on their unwitting wives.

GIRLS TODAY

"When I was a child times were very different," related Harriet Tuctness. "I was born in 1849 and celebrated my fourth birthday in a covered wagon while we were crossing the Plains.

"Upon our arrival in the Willamette Valley, Father took up a donation land claim and built a log cabin. My older sister and I helped Father. We drove the team, broadcast seeds, weeded, irrigated and when it was time for harvest we gathered the wheat and oats and shocked it in bundles. We milked the cows, fed the chickens and did whatever other chores were necessary.

"Mother finally put her foot down and said she did not want her girls to be simple farm hands. So in addition to our outside work we learned to do women's work; cooking, weaving, making soap, spinning wool, keeping a house and things such as that.

"My mother tanned deer hides and made buckskin gloves. And she was a master hand at making shoes. I never had a pair of store-bought shoes 'til I was full grown. Mother taught us how to wash the wool from our sheep, card it and spin it into thread. We used the wool thread to knit socks. The socks were sold for fifty cents a pair and were accepted at stores as legal tender, the same as beaver pelts, sacks of wheat or gold dust.

"Girls of my generation were instructed in the important things in life; how to sacrifice and work hard in hopes of a better future. My, but times have certainly changed. Young women of today cannot even knit a wool sock, nor, for that matter can very many of them manage to cook a decent meal. Instead of labor they are content to idle away their existence riding around in automobiles and playing contract bridge. I look at this coming generation of young women and ask myself what, oh what, will become of this world?"

THE DRESS

Emily Hunsaker and Eliza Gordon were best friends. Their families had come west together, settled on adjoining land claims and built a single, two-room log cabin that straddled the property line. One day while the two women worked and visited, the conversation turned to how long it had been since either of them had had a new dress. They concluded it had been a long, long time and resolved to do something about it.

"I have an idea how we can raise money for material," said Emily. "There are very few laying hens around and yet all our neighbors want fresh eggs and meat. We shall raise chickens."

"How can we afford foundation stock?" asked Eliza.

"Soap," offered Emily with firm conviction. "Even though it is hard work and does not pay a great deal we shall make soap, sell it and save every cent."

From the sale of soap the two women earned enough to purchase a hen and rooster. They built a laying nest on the back of the cabin, lined it with dry grasses and waited. Before long the hen was setting on a clutch of eggs. After a few months the women had earned enough from their chickens to purchase a few yards of material. Eliza insisted that Emily, since it had been her idea, would have the first dress. They worked together to make a fine garment and Emily told her friend, "I shall wear it for the first time on Sunday."

On Saturday morning Emily washed her new dress on a scrub board, rinsed it in spring water and hung it on the line to dry in the wind. Later she happened to glance outside and, to her horror, discovered one of the cows had pulled her new dress down in the mud and was chewing on it. She flew through the doorway and ran the cow away but the damage was done. The dress was ruined.

YEAR OF THE GRASSHOPPER

The summer of 1874 was perfect for growing crops. The grain was ready to cut, the hay was thick and green, and there was an abundance of vegetables and berries. Everyone had high hopes for a record harvest.

"On the first day of August there came a haze. The sun was veiled. It seemed as if we were in for a storm—and then grasshoppers began dropping to earth," remembered Mary Lyons.

"They devoured every green thing, eating the leaves and twigs off our young fruit trees, and seemed to relish the green peaches on the trees; but strangely they left the pits hanging. I thought to save some of my garden by covering it with gunny sacks, but the hoppers regarded that as a huge joke and enjoyed the awning thus provided; or if they could not get under, they ate their way through. The cabbage and lettuce disappeared the first afternoon; by the next day they had eaten the onions. They had an interesting way of eating onions. They devoured the tops, and then ate all of the onions from the inside, leaving only the outer shell. When the crops and the garden were devoured the grasshoppers invaded our home, and on retiring we had to shake the bugs out of the bedding, and were fortunate if we did not have to make a second raid before morning."

Eventually the grasshoppers moved on, leaving the countryside reeking with their offensive odor. Livestock that had consumed the locusts—the chickens, turkeys and hogs—tasted so strongly they were inedible. Even worse was the fact that the insects had laid eggs before departing and the following spring the young grasshoppers emerged. This time they moved on quickly and the farmers were able to replant. They brought in a record crop the fall of 1875.

MOTHER

Grandmother was telling the younger generation about the Great Depression. "It was my mother, your great-grandmother, who held our family together. I remember her telling us children, 'You'll just have to make do.' We soon learned that meant doing without.

"Along about Thanksgiving I would drag out the Sears, Roebuck & Co. catalog. Mother would suggest Santa might bring me only a single present and that I should not be terribly disappointed if it was not something I wanted. One year I got a new blouse and another I got a blouse and skirt.

"I lost count of the number of times we begged Mother for a nickel for candy; but her reply, after an exasperated sigh, was always the same, 'You know money doesn't grow on trees.'

"We grew a big garden, had chickens and a milk cow and raised our own meat. For extra money, sometimes the only money, we sold cream and butter. We never lacked food on our table. It did not bother me being poor because all my friends were poor, too.

"For fun we used to play baseball in the pasture. And we held impromptu games like Kick the Can, Annie Annie Over, King of the Manure Pile, or engaged in a spirited Cow Chip Toss. In those days you made your own fun.

"Mother had very little fun. She washed clothes on a scrub board, ironed with a flat iron heated on the wood stove, cooked, baked, canned, milked and took care of us kids. Dad farmed and worked out whenever he found a paying job.

"Years later I tried to tell Mother how much I admired her courage but she brushed it aside, saying, 'All I did was what had to be done.'"

LADY'S MAN

Cherokee Bob was born to a white father and an Indian mother. He never felt as though he fit in the social structure of the East Coast and at an early age he ventured west and tried his hand at mining, gambling and living life free and easy.

In Walla Walla, Washington, Cherokee Bob attended a performance by a traveling theatrical company. A group of soldiers in the audience began calling to a pretty actress, whistling when she tried to speak her lines and making loud, coarse comments. Cherokee Bob rose to his feet and admonished the men, "You are interrupting the performance and the lady does not appreciate your unwelcome attention."

He returned to his seat and the soldiers persisted. The second time Cherokee Bob got to his feet, his guns were blazing. Before he finished, six of the soldiers lay dead. Cherokee Bob immediately left town, heading into the mountains toward the mining town of Florence, Idaho.

Once again trouble found him and, as before, a woman was at the root of the difficulty. Cherokee Bob was spending time with one of the saloon girls when Jack Williams, a hot-headed gambler, returned to town and claimed she was his girl. He challenged Cherokee Bob to a gunfight.

When Cherokee Bob stepped into the street he had no inkling that his weapons had been tampered with by the woman whose favor he was trying to win. Jack Williams made his move. Cherokee Bob reacted out of instinct and cleared leather first, but when he pulled the trigger his revolver did not fire. Jack Williams gunned him down.

On a hillside above the mining settlement of Florence is a rotting plank that serves as a grave marker for Cherokee Bob; the miner, the gambler, the lawless troublemaker. But above all, he was a lady's man.

A LONG WAY HOME

One morning in the spring of 1924 Mary Smith, a widow, opened her back door and found an emaciated dog lying on her back porch. She cried out, "Oh! My poor darling," as she swept up the dog and carried him inside.

The dog's coat was matted with dirt, briars and thorns. When Mary saw that the pads of his feet were worn away to bone she cried and said, "You must have come a very long way, a very long way indeed."

Mary cared for the dog. She soaked and cleaned his paws, dried them with a warm towel and applied several layers of paraffin to seal them. She brushed his coat and washed him. While she was nursing the dog she hummed and sang him tender lullabies. He would not eat, but lapped a small amount of water and that seemed to revive him.

Late that afternoon the dog rose and made his way to the back door. Mary opened the door and watched as the dog hobbled stiffly down the steps, along the walkway and through the open gate to the street. Without looking back he turned south and continued on his way.

Mary saw the dog one more time. That was after he had become famous. Newspapers related the story of a dog that had become lost in Illinois and made his way home to Silverton, Oregon, a distance of nearly 3,000 miles. He was heralded as "Bobby the Wonder Dog" and when he was put on display in Portland a crowd of several thousand people came to visit the remarkable dog. Mary attended the festivities and when she came near, Bobby gave a high-pitched bark and rushed to her, rewarding her with wet kisses of thanks.

ARRANGED MARRIAGE

"I was born in 1852, near what would become the town of Kettle Falls, Washington," stated Mary Gendron. "My father, a French-Canadian from Montreal, trapped along the little creeks that emptied into the Columbia River.

"We grew a little grain that was ground for flour and we always raised a big garden. But mostly we existed on wild meat. There was plenty of game for the taking—deer, bear, and partridge. Life was not difficult. In fact, there was not a single time when we went hungry for lack of being able to obtain food.

"Nearly all the settlers who came to that area were French or French-Canadian. They talked about making wine but the weather and the altitude did not allow grapes to be grown there. Father had to purchase brandy from the Hudson's Bay Company store instead. On those occasions when we visited the store, the men would drink whiskey and brandy and sing old songs or tell tales of their hunting and trapping experiences. For a time the children would be allowed to listen but before the evening was very old we would be trundled off to bed.

"In those days our roads were nothing more than trails that wound around through the woods. Every Sunday morning our family rode horseback to the mission for mass. Afterward nearly everyone in the congregation went fishing. We had some gay times there on the river.

"It was the French custom that when a girl reached marrying age her parents would arrange a match. I was 14 years old when I was introduced to the man I would marry. He was 21 years older than me. After knowing him for one week we were engaged and a few days later we married."

PERFECT AS A PICTURE

Ella and Alfred and their six children lived on a hardscrabble South Dakota homestead. One day, less than a week from the due date of her seventh child, Ella left the children at home with Alfred and walked a mile to the neighbor's house. She visited with her friend Greta and stayed through supper. As the two women were washing dishes, Greta asked, "What is wrong? Something is wrong, isn't it?"

Ella broke into tears. She sobbed, "My baby's comin' an' won't have a thing to wear; clothes, diapers, blankets. All we got are a bunch of threadbare hand-me-downs that should have been throwed away...."

"Now, now," comforted Greta. "I've got some extra material. We'll just get to work and fix you up."

Greta searched through her material pile, setting aside several yards of colorful flannel, leftover cotton from her boys' shirts and a flour sack. Then the women went to work. They made little shirts for a boy and dresses for a girl. They made blankets and diapers, too. They visited and laughed and enjoyed the evening.

It was close to midnight when Ella announced she had to be going. Greta insisted on walking her home. Along the way Ella stopped and hugged Greta, thanking her for being such a true friend. And there, under the canopy of the prairie sky and the vast Milky Way, she confided, "I was feeling so alone, so desperate, that if you hadn't been home, I was gonna end it."

The baby arrived on schedule and was greeted with a collection of new gowns and little shirts and flannel blankets with lace around the edges. Ella sat in the old rocking chair, rocking back and forth, singing softly to the bundle in her arms and it was as perfect as a picture.

BURIED ALIVE

Sarah Winnemucca was a member of the nomadic Paiute tribe of the High Desert. She was a young girl when the first white people arrived. Sarah recalled, "My grandfather, Chief Truckee, stood and clasped his hands together and greeted them, 'My white brothers have come at last!'

"When our white brothers left they gave my grandfather a tin plate—it was so bright. My grandfather called for all his people to come together and he showed them the beautiful gift. Everyone was pleased. Nothing like it was ever seen before. My grandfather bored holes in it, fastened it on his head, and wore it as a hat.

"Every year after that there was more and more white emigrants. Rumors began to circulate among my people because of fearful news coming from different tribes. It was said white people were stealing Indian children and eating them. Soon we were all afraid of white people. Every dust that we could see blowing in the valley we would say it was the white people coming to eat us.

"What a fright we all got one morning to hear white people were near. My aunt and my mother said, 'We must bury our girls, or they shall be eaten up.' So they buried us, placing sagebrush over our faces so we could breathe.

"Can anyone imagine my feelings being buried alive, thinking every minute that I was to be unburied and eaten by the people my grandfather had loved so much? With my heart throbbing we lay there all day. At last we heard some whispering and footsteps coming nearer and nearer. Then I saw my mother and she cried out, 'Here they are!' And we were safe."

YOUNG BRIDE

"We were suffering through another long winter when Father got hold of a pamphlet that touted, in the most glowing terms, all the attributes of the far West," recalled Melvina Millican. "In the spring we joined a wagon train heading out from Independence, Missouri.

"We had two good wagons, five yoke of oxen and provisions of bacon, ham, corn meal, dried apples, beans, coffee and, as we brought our cows along, plenty of milk and butter. And as soon as we struck the Platte River we had all the buffalo and antelope meat we could eat.

"We crossed the Rocky Mountains and the Blue Mountains and upon reaching the Columbia River, Father and some of the other men cut down trees, sawed them into planks and built flatboats. On our trip through the rapids of the Columbia one of the boats tipped over and a boy and two men were drowned.

"When we reached the west side of the Cascades Father took up a donation land claim and built a log cabin. He left an open place in the roof for the smoke to go out and put up some pole beds for us to sleep in.

"At that time there were very few white women living in the far West and even fewer single white women. Those who were eligible for marriage were in much demand by the mountain men who lived there as well as the single men who were arriving and claiming homestead land. One of my chums was married when she was 12 years old. Mother thought that was awful young and made me promise to wait until I was at least 13. And so, even though I had my share of suitors, I delayed making any commitment until two days after my thirteenth birthday. Then I married."

16

SUNDAY BEST

"One of our neighbors sold out and we bought one of his cows. That is where this story begins," related Fannie Holsinger.

"The cow had a calf and I went to the lower pasture to find it. But the cow found me instead and chased me over the fence. After that I was nervous around that cow so my husband built a small rail pen. The first time I went to try and milk the cow I ran her into this pen and asked my husband to stand guard. He could not milk as he had a crippled right arm.

"The milking was proceeding, and I had just remarked how wonderful the flow of milk was, when the angry cow managed to hook me with a leg and drag me inside the pen. I do remember the feel of her maddened breath on my face and seeing those terrible horns trying to gore me. Then there was nothing but blackness.

"As I later learned, my husband dragged me from under the vicious cow and tossed me over the rails. He was clubbed furiously before he could extricate himself. He thought I was dead but I managed to escape with bruises the full length of my body. I told him to sell the cow, that I would not dare try to milk that insane animal.

"The worst part of my ordeal was that someone mentioned the incident to a newspaper reporter. He wrote up a story and it was illustrated with a picture of a regular movie-type beauty being tossed over a board fence. One of my neighbors looked at that and sniffed, 'Well there's your problem, looks to me like you must have put on your Sunday best to milk.'"

A WOMAN'S SUCCESS

Luzena Wilson, her husband and two small children arrived in Nevada City, California soon after gold had been discovered. While miners around them were striking it rich the Wilsons took time, for the sake of the children, to hew logs, split shakes and build a shelter.

Luzena related, "As soon as our cabin was built my husband went off prospecting and I cast about for some plan to assist in the recuperation of our family finances. It occurred to me that many of the miners in Nevada City were in need of a place to stay and food to eat. I managed to purchase canvas on credit and fashion it into a tent. I also tacked together a long table and benches. And even though they were terribly expensive, I was able to purchase provisions at a neighboring store and promptly set about cooking a delicious meal.

"When my husband returned he found, amid the light of pine torches, twenty miners eating at my table. Each man paid me a dollar. That was encouragement enough for my husband and he joined me as a partner in this prospering enterprise.

"The money continued to pour in and we built a house, enlarging it a room at a time as we could afford it. Before long we had two hundred boarders living with us. They were perfectly content to pay $25 per week for that privilege. Within a short amount of time we had amassed something over $20,000.

"But one night a fire swept through Nevada City and wiped us out. The remnant of our fortune consisted of the pocket change my husband was carrying at the time, $500. We used that to start all over again and the second time we were just as successful as we had been the first time."

HARD LUCK LIFE

Sarah Jenkins had a hard luck life. At the age of 16 she married Andrew Jackson Masters and the following year, in 1843, they started west from Missouri with the first wagon train to travel the Oregon Trail.

As they neared the Methodist Mission at The Dalles, Sarah went into labor and gave birth to a baby boy. They remained at the mission while Andrew traveled on to the Willamette Valley. The following spring he returned for his wife and son, transporting them down the Columbia River by canoe. Along the way the canoe capsized and the Masters family was thrown into the water. They were lucky to escape with their lives.

They took up residence in a log cabin in the Willamette Valley. Here their second child was born. When gold was discovered at Sutters Fort in 1848, Andrew decided the family should go to California and make their fortune. But after a single day of prospecting Andrew told Sarah, "Mucking gravel is not for me. Tomorrow we start back for home."

"You dragged me all this way to make a fortune and I will not leave until we have done so," Sarah advised him. Within a year they had enough money to return to Oregon. They traveled north by ship and all went well until they reached the Columbia River bar and their ship ran aground. The crew and passengers were saved but they lost all their possessions. Once again the Masters were forced to start from scratch. This time they took a donation land claim and by 1856 there were five children in the family. That year Andrew quarreled with a neighbor and the neighbor killed him.

Sarah remained on the farm. She did the chores, harvested the crops and raised her children. In time she married Henry Willoughby and had three more children.

PATRIOTIC LADY

The Civil War was fought in the east but one mild skirmish did occur 3,000 miles away in Jacksonville, Oregon.

When fighting broke out, Jacksonville was split between Confederate sympathizers and those strongly in favor of the Union cause. The battle in Jacksonville was fought the morning the citizens awoke to find that a pole had been erected and a rebel flag was fluttering in a stiff breeze.

Leaders hastily called a town meeting. A merchant was the first to speak and he declared, "We can't have such a thing flying over our town. What will folks think?"

"Let 'em think what they will," claimed a Confederate miner.

The two sides argued back and forth. At times it seemed a fistfight, or worse, was inevitable but then cooler heads prevailed. A compromise was finally suggested—the Confederate flag would stay and another flagpole, flying the Stars and Stripes, would be erected across the street.

Aunty Ganung, wife of the town doctor Louis Ganung, took matters into her own hands. She grabbed a pistol and an axe and marched to the flagpole. She laid down the pistol and lifted the axe. With the practiced swing of a logger she chopped down the pole. It tumbled onto the dusty street.

The men stood in stunned silence as Aunty Ganung gathered up the flag in her arms, took hold of the pistol and walked past them on her way home. Never again did a Confederate flag fly over Jacksonville.

PRACTICAL EXPERIENCE

"My folks' philosophy of education was that a person was never supposed to quit learning. But they were never real big on a traditional book-learning education," stated Martha Gilliam.

"What formal learning I did receive began the year after we had come west and settled on our land claim. A friend of Father's visited our cabin and told me I should learn to read and write. He whittled the letters of the alphabet with his jackknife on a smooth-grained shake and I practiced writing the letters using bullet lead to make my marks.

"I went one month to Mr. Green's school and two months more to Mr. McCarty's log cabin school. He taught us to read by tearing pages from a Bible; there was no other written material in the country. When you could read your page you traded with a classmate. The only school book I ever owned was an ABC primer.

"My schooling was cut short by Father's death in 1847. He was killed fighting in the Cayuse Indian War. Our family had a pretty hard time for a while but Mother was a good worker and we managed to get along.

"I was 10 years old, plenty old enough to do my share. I drove the oxen and my brother held the plow. When we harvested we cut the wheat with a reap hook, tramped it out with the cattle and cleaned it by throwing it up in the air and letting the afternoon breeze blow away the chaff. It was my job to grind the wheat. Mother baked twice a week and it took a lot of grinding to keep us in whole wheat flour.

"When I was young there was never time for much book learning. Mostly my education came from nothing more than practical experience."

THE BUFFALO STAMPEDE

In the spring of 1847 the Markham family joined a wagon train of friends and neighbors headed for the Promise Land out west. Many fascinating stories were told about that trip but none could compare to the one concerning Mrs. Markham and the buffalo.

The incident occurred out on the plains. The wagon train had camped near a small stream. While the men cared for the livestock, Mrs Markham, who was always concerned about clean water, took two pails and hiked a distance from camp.

On the return leg she thought she heard thunder. She set the pails on the ground and searched the sky, but no clouds were in sight. However, the sound of rolling thunder was unmistakable and growing louder.

Suddenly Mrs. Markham realized the noise was the rumbling of stampeding buffalo. She hurried toward the distant circle of wagons, packing the buckets, water sloshing over the rims. At the sight of buffalo boiling over the top of the ridge she dropped the buckets and started to run. It appeared she might stay beyond the edge of the herd, but she stumbled and fell and in the next instant she became part of the surging brown mass. Hooves flashed and choking dust boiled around her.

After the herd passed Mr. Markham ran to where he had last seen his wife. He found her unconscious, suffering a broken shoulder and several cracked ribs. She was bruised and bleeding from many cuts and had lost nearly all her clothes; but she was alive. In later years she never tired of telling her story of being caught in a buffalo stampede and surviving the ordeal.

THE HANGING

"I was visiting my grandmother when word came around that Daniel Delaney had been murdered," recalled Kate Miller. "Even though I was quite young I was acquainted with Mr. Delaney because in those days folks would stop and visit with neighbors.

"Mr. Delaney had come west in the early days and took a land claim south of Salem. As far as I know he was a lone man without a family. He was quite elderly, at least 70 years old.

"In those days there was no crime to speak of and that was what made it so difficult to conceive of the fact anyone would kill Mr. Delaney. But kill him they did, and in a most brutal fashion. Two fellows who had just come into the country beat Mr. Delaney to death.

"A few months later, while I was walking to school with some of my girl friends, we saw men building a platform. We inquired what they were doing. They told us they were constructing a gallows on which the men responsible for killing Mr. Delaney were to be hanged. Well, that certainly gave me a sudden case of the shivers.

"The day for the public execution was May 17, 1865. As the time drew near, the excitement built until it actually became something of a social event. Folks drove their wagons, piled high with kids, twenty miles or more to watch. I never considered attending the hanging. Even the thought of it turned my stomach. But I did go close enough to see the crowd assembled along Mill Creek. It was a big crowd, as big as a circus would have brought out. But it turned out this gathering was a lot quieter than a circus crowd."

THAT ONE TIME

"In the early years the Indians were friendly, often visiting our homestead and bringing us gifts of salmon and venison. Since there were practically no white people in that part of the country, I played with Indian children. I soon learned to speak their jargon and we had a jolly time together," remembered Ida Davis.

"Over time the Indians suffered many wrongs and injustices at the hands of white settlers. But we never had any trouble until one time when Father had to go to the settlement to get provisions, a trip that took the best part of ten days. He left Mother and us children alone at home.

"While he was gone a large number of Indians visited and once they discovered Father was not around they began making threats. They said, 'White people come, steal our land. We will kill you!'

"Mother never wavered. She stood tall and told the Indians, 'I cannot prevent you from killing me. I have no way to defend myself. But before you do, I want you to promise me one thing. I want you to kill my children first because I cannot bear to think of them being left motherless.'

"She pushed us out in front of her. We stood there looking up at the Indians. I remember their faces were painted. I was terribly afraid.

"The warriors did not have the stomach to kill children and soon departed. The following day they returned and this time they brought pine nuts, fish and huckleberries. One Indian told Mother that she was very brave and that as long as his tribe was in that part of the country they would always protect us. Ever after we never had a lick of trouble with the Indians."

FATHER

Nina Parr remembers the Great Depression. "We lived on beans and mostly did without. But it was Father who suffered the most during those dark days."

Mr. Parr owned a grocery store, a wholesale produce business and operated a fleet of delivery trucks. But soon after the stock market crash of 1929 his customers began to default on their bills. Creditors swooped in and took the grocery store and the wholesale produce company.

Mr. Parr clung to his trucking business, selling the trucks one at a time to pay the most pressing bills. Nina recalled, "Father was a proud man, a very proud man. He always told us, 'If your word's no good, you're no good.' And since he had given his word, he felt obligated to pay every bill he owed, even though his customers did not hold themselves to such a high moral road."

One day Nina overheard her father tell her mother that he could no longer walk down the street and hold his head up. He said he owed money to every man he met and that he felt his only recourse was to go down to the river and never come back.

Hearing her father so distraught scared Nina. She went to her bedroom, dressed in her best clothes, packed a few necessities and sneaked out of the house. She caught a ride into town where she went from business to business asking for work. That night she called home with the news she had found a job working in a doctor's office.

Nina saved four dollars and sent it to her father, so he could come to town and look for work. "I was so proud to give him the money," she said, "but I'll be darned if on the way someone didn't pick his pocket and steal the four dollars. That was the lowest point. From there, gradually, very gradually, times got better."

HUNTING STORIES

"Our neighbors, two brothers named Tom and Jack, were notorious for hunting out of season. Not that all of us homesteaders didn't take wild game from time to time, but Tom and Jack made a career out of poaching," Grandma told.

"One time the state sent in a game warden. Tom and Jack had several deer hanging in a tree so the meat would cool. According to the story that made the rounds this game warden came riding in. A warning shot was fired. But the warden paid no mind and kept right on coming. Tom, who was a terrific marksman, made the next shot count. He shot the saddle horn off the warden's saddle. I suspect that was a little too close for comfort. The warden promptly turned his horse around and was never seen around these parts again.

"Another time Jack killed a nice buck way back in the bush. It just happened to be during hunting season. He was standing there beside the dead deer, contemplating how he was going to transport it to the road, when a state police officer stepped from behind a yellow-bellied pine and said, 'I sure hope you've got a valid tag for this buck.'

"Tom pulled out his wallet and started thumbing through it, claiming, 'I think I got one — I remember I was fixin' to get one — I must have misplaced it.'

"The officer finally told Jack that he was going to write him up and Tom replied, 'Do what you have to do. Suppose you're gonna confiscate my buck, too. Well, then you're just gonna have to pack it outta here.'

"The state policeman threw the buck over his shoulders and, staggering under the weight, made his way out. When they got to the road Jack reached in his shirt pocket, saying as he did, 'Just remembered where I put that darn tag. Why here it is!'"

TYPICAL UPBRINGING

"I was born and raised on our donation land claim," related Sarah Booth. "Father was a traveling preacher, gone much of the time, so it fell to Mother to oversee the farm, raise all of us kids and take care of the household chores. In those days there were no labor-saving conveniences. Mother carded and spun the wool. She knitted socks and mittens, molded candles, cooked over the fireplace. I well remember the hours I spent sitting beside her while she sewed clothes, by hand, for all of us.

"Our neighbors were Indians. One of the Indian boys, his name was Moses, became very good friends with my brothers. They used to hunt and fish together. One day Moses ran to our house and, in a very excited manner, informed us that bad Indians were headed in our direction and if we did not leave immediately, they would kill us

"Mother was greatly alarmed at this frightful news. We hurried away and spent the night at a neighbor's house. The next morning we returned home and discovered moccasin tracks all around our house but the Indians had not burned it and everything was intact.

"Another time an Indian brought to our house a white silk shawl with long fringes. It was so very beautiful. I was crazy to have it. But in spite of my ardent desire Mother absolutely refused to trade for it.

"After the Indian had gone she explained her actions, saying she felt it would be improper for a minister's daughter to saunter about with such an expensive silk shawl around her shoulders, that it might give folks the wrong impression.

"Thinking back, I would have to say my brothers and sisters and I had a pretty typical upbringing."

HOMESTEADING MOTHER

When the Homestead Act promising free land was passed into law, Ida and Lawrence Girton decided to pull up stakes in Ohio and move west. They found a spot to their liking on the High Desert and laid claim to 320 acres. Lawrence built a two-story house on the homestead with a split shake roof, horizontal siding, glass windows and a covered back porch. The outdoor privy was located a short distance away. Lawrence dug a root cellar and a well. He built a barn with milking stanchions, stock pens and a chicken coop.

But the Girtons soon realized the homestead was not capable of providing enough income for a growing family. When the fourth child arrived Lawrence began working outside, using the team and wagon to haul freight. Ida stayed at home, caring for the children, milking the cows and tending a big garden.

To break the monotony of everyday life Ida took up photography. She found a special offer for trays and supplies to develop her own photographs in the "Monkey Wards" catalog and ordered the complete package. On moonless nights she developed her pictures, documenting the Girtons' homesteading years.

Ida was well known among her neighbors because of her immaculate housekeeping skills. Years after the Girtons moved off their homestead one of Ida's daughters revealed the secret of her mother's success. According to the daughter Ida could see neighbors coming across the desert from two miles away, and she would quickly scrub the white pine floors with hot lye water. By the time the neighbor arrived the floor would have dried and it would be spotlessly clean.

MIRACLE

The summer of 1933 was a miserable time. On the national front the country was held tightly in the grip of the worst depression in history. Locally, farmers were suffering from an extended drought. Just when it seemed things could not get any worse, a hot wind began to blow. It blew for weeks on end and scoured away the topsoil, and with it the farmers' last shred of hope.

At this low point a traveling preacher arrived and pitched his revival tent next to the grange hall. Word spread and families from all the neighboring farms began to congregate and pray for better times. The preacher realized he could never hope to win souls with conditions being what they were and on the last night of the revival he called out to those in attendance, "Sing *There Shall Be Showers of Blessings.* Sing all four verses."

At the conclusion of the song the preacher called out, "Sing it again." This time when the singing ended there was an ominous quiet. The wind had stopped blowing and then, from far away, the soft rumble of thunder could be distinguished. A moment later the first drop of rain pinged against the stretched canvas, followed by a barrage of raindrops. Again, the preacher urged the congregation, "Keep singing!"

The congregation sang loudly, and they hugged one another and tears of joy ran unashamedly down their cheeks. They called praise to the Lord while the rain came harder, settling the dust and charging the air with sweet, pungent smells.

Never was there a better revival. Never were more souls saved. Folks claimed that while they were singing, God had brought them a miracle.

SHORTCUT

In 1853 a small group of pioneers veered away from the Oregon Trail at Fort Walla Walla and sought to find a way across the Cascade Mountains to Puget Sound.

When they reached the mountains the men fell the tall timber and the women and children followed, hacking at the undergrowth and the small saplings, cutting them close to the ground so the wagons could pass. Mile after grudging mile they pushed on, clearing a road, knowing that if they failed the snow would come and they would die in the mountains.

Struggling over the divide and starting down the west side they found the way blocked by a rocky cliff. One man in the wagon train had a 180-foot rope that was stout enough to let the wagons down the steep slope but it was not nearly long enough. It was suggested that the poorest ox be slaughtered and its green hide cut into strips and braided into a rope. The ox was killed and the rope made but it was still not long enough. Three more oxen had to be slaughtered before the rope would reach to the bottom of the incline.

While the makeshift rope was fastened around a tree at the top of the incline, and each wagon was lowered down the face of the cliff, two men were sent ahead to scout the way and blaze a trail. After several days they stumbled into the Hudson's Bay Company post at Fort Nisqually.

The fur traders formed a rescue party and when they reached the pioneers they distributed a large quantity of food and supplies and led them safely through to Fort Nisqually.

THE RIDE

The stagecoach was designed to provide a convenient way for a woman to travel but all too often it was found to be a grueling journey over rocky and rutted roads, through stormy weather, with unforseen danger lurking around every bend.

Carrie Sterns wrote of her stagecoach ride: "At the stage station we passengers were crowded in—wedged in would better express the arrangement—the coach. Our route was by no means the shortest distance between settlements. We diverged here and there for the delivery of mail or the fording of streams.

"At dusk we reached the hotel where we were to lay over. It was a rude, rambling one-story affair and soon after supper, when fairly abed and about to fall asleep, the sounds of fiddles in the dining room told that a country dance was beginning. Though very tired, the fiddles, the stamping of stoutly shod feet on the rough floor, and perhaps the excitement attendant on new experiences, kept me awake until 3 a.m., and it seemed I had only caught the merest wink of sleep after dancing ceased when loud knocking at my door and 'Stage leaving!' aroused me.

"When I reached the stage door I discovered that every seat was taken. I lifted my eyes to the driver's seat and managed to ask, 'May I sit with you?'

"He called down to me, 'Why sure you can.'

"I was pulled and hoisted to the seat and away we dashed. I was fairly holding my breath and tightly gripping the railing at the end of my seat. But the sensation of swift motion and aloftness, the keen air of the October morning's dawn, the unusualness and the unexpectedness of that phase of my journey—it was truly intoxicating!"

THE EARLY DAYS

"We were among the first white settlers along the North Pacific coast, taking up residence on Whidby Island," stated Flora Engle. "We endured what folks of the present generation would most likely consider extreme hardships.

"To give an example of this, I remember a fellow from our settlement journeyed to the other side of the island and upon his return he was asked about conditions and replied that he did not see much difference. 'Over there they have salmon and potatoes,' he said, 'while here we have venison and potatoes.'

"Hunting deer was scarcely considered sport, for the deer were so tame they often strayed into our back yards. To break the monotony of our venison diet a farmer would occasionally kill a beef and share the meat with his neighbors who later, in turn, would return an equal and like quantity of beef. Flour was in short supply. At one barn-raising, of all of the men who attended and carried their dinners, only one had bread and that was in the form of a rather dry biscuit.

"Homes were scantily furnished as nearly all furniture had to be shipped around the Horn, transferred to another sailing vessel at San Francisco, and brought north to our island. The arrival of one of these vessels was always welcomed for most carried supplies of many sorts and these were sold or traded to local settlers.

"The most serious problem we faced in those early years arose from the wolves that would venture forth from the forest and devour sheep, pigs and calves. The practice of spreading strychnine on the carcasses of deer finally resulted in the complete extermination of the wolves. I believe the last wolf was killed in 1858. After that we did not have to fear these fierce predators."

WENT TO KANSAS

Miriam Davis was born the twelfth child of a poor family living in the state of New York. She married young and she and her husband, William Colt, had two children, Willie and Mema. By all accounts the family lived an idyllic life—until the day William announced he wished to uproot the family and move west to Kansas.

Three months after loading their belongings into a covered wagon and starting west, Miriam wrote from the road: "The water is very bad here; a green scum covers the top of it; have made tea of it and cooked rice in it and my darling children are so thirsty they must drink this water, that is so full of disease."

Soon after William became ill and the following day they could not travel. Miriam walked to a nearby farm to beg for food. She wrote of the experience: "I could hardly realize that I was gazing upon the home comforts of chairs, tables and plenty of food. The good lady was just taking a loaf of wheat bread from a Dutch oven ... the largest loaf of bread that I have ever seen."

That evening little Willie became violently ill with fever and chills. At last he cried out for an apple, and then he stopped breathing. Ten days later William passed on.

Miriam buried her son and husband. She sold the wagon and stock to the homesteader and, along with her daughter, returned to New York. Miriam wrote a book entitled, *Went to Kansas*. It was published in 1862 and from it Miriam earned a measure of fame and enough money to support herself and her daughter.

HORSE QUEEN

Kit Wilkins was born in 1857. She managed to parlay a teenage interest in horses into a stake in the Wilkins Company, a sprawling horse ranch that eventually extended into three states—Oregon, Idaho and Nevada.

As the Wilkins Company holdings increased, Kit registered the Diamond brand and hired more cowboys to help with the roundups. At one point it was estimated that 20,000 head of horses roamed the Wilkins Company range. Every two weeks a trainload of mustangs was rounded up and shipped to markets in the east.

Kit was described by one of the cowboys who rode for her as "a beautiful, blue-eyed blonde who rode a palomino horse the same color as her hair. Her saddle, bridle, and other trappings were mounted in silver and gold. She made quite a splendid sight coming through the sagebrush."

Kit never thought of herself as above the level of the common cowboy. She rode the range and got dirty and sweaty along with the men she employed. She could handle a rope with the best of them and when the mood struck her she crawled on the back of an outlaw mustang and rode it until it quit bucking.

During World War I there was a great demand for remounts and Kit sold horses to both the United States and the French governments. But she knew the good times would never last and advised her cowboys that times were changing, that the world was in the middle of a mechanical revolution and she predicted horses would become almost worthless.

Kit took her own advice. One day she up and sold her holdings and retired to Glenns Ferry, Idaho. Until the day she died, cowboys drifting through the country would swing by Glenns Ferry to visit with the woman known far and wide as the "Horse Queen of the West."

THE LONE INDIAN

"As we traveled west by wagon we had some thrilling experiences," related Elmira Whitaker. "We left Missouri early in the spring of 1852 and not until October did we finally land at Fort Vancouver.

"The most trying time of our journey occurred after a member of our party, a woman, came down with a serious illness. George Miller served as captain of our wagon train and was both a knowledgeable and courageous man. He advised the sick woman's family that it would be best if they would lay over a day or two. And since we were in Indian country he offered to stay with them, calling for volunteers who would do likewise.

"According to the story Mr. Miller later related, the Indians soon descended on the lone wagon and demanded food. Having spent considerable time in Indian country, Mr. Miller knew the consequences of refusing such a request. Food was set out and the Indians ate until most of the provisions for the long journey had been devoured. Very little of any value remained and soon the Indians departed, all except for one warrior.

"At length this lone Indian made ready to leave. He insisted upon shaking hands with everyone. When he clasped hands with one of the young sons of the sick woman, he tried to pull the boy to his horse. I suppose he would have stolen the lad except for Mr. Miller's quick action, tearing loose the Indian's grip and ordering him from camp.

"The oxen were yoked and the party hurried west to catch up to the wagon train. As the small group neared the safety of our main camp, the lone Indian, who had followed them every step of the way, simply turned his horse away and was never seen again."

UNUSUAL PET

"I am from pioneering stock," Mrs. Charles Olson said. "My father, Benjamin Barlow, crossed the Plains by wagon in 1852 and settled on a donation land claim on the lower Columbia River.

"When I was a child I remember Father setting nets to catch salmon. He made his own nets. In a box nailed to the wall near the fireplace he kept the oak wood needles and the material and on long evenings he worked at making nets. I helped him by threading the needles.

"Father netted salmon at three different eddies. There were so very many salmon in those days and also a great many seals that assembled to feast on the salmon. Father would shoot as many as he could but it never seemed to make much of a dent in the seal population.

"One day while Father was running the nets he found a tiny baby seal caught in one of them. He put it in his boat and brought it back to show us children. We, of course, begged to keep it so Father filled Mother's wash tub with water, made a pen around it and we put the little seal in there. It whimpered and cried like a lost puppy. At first we fed it milk but as it grew older we fed it fish.

"The seal was soon too large for the wash tub. Father said we must turn it loose. We tried putting it in the river but each time it climbed out, crawled up the bank and beat us back to the house.

"At last Father put the seal in his boat. We stood on the hill and watched him row far down the river where he set it adrift. That was the last we ever saw of our unusual pet."

SHIP OF MYSTERY

Several dozen women were destined to became widows that fateful day in November 1875 when the *Sunshine*, a three-masted schooner, headed out from San Francisco harbor. She was on the return leg of her maiden voyage, bound for Marshfield, Oregon.

The crew diligently worked to stretch the new canvas and when the ship came to, the sails billowed and the sleek, copper-clad hull cut through the choppy waters like a sharp knife. Reaching the open ocean Captain Bennet, a fine ship builder and trusted skipper, turned north.

That was the last anyone saw of the *Sunshine* until three weeks later when her battered hull washed ashore on a spit of land twenty miles north of the Columbia River. She quickly settled into the shifting sand and no bodies were ever recovered.

Rumors circulated that the *Sunshine* had been carrying a large treasure chest. The owner of the vessel confirmed that nearly forty pounds of gold had been aboard. More rumors surfaced. One report claimed several of the passengers had murdered the captain and crew, stolen the gold and escaped in a lifeboat. A man who claimed to have been an eyewitness said he watched the *Sunshine* run aground and saw the crew abandon ship and bury a strong box on shore.

The captain, crew and the passengers were listed as lost at sea. None of the men ever returned to their wives. And to this day the mystery of the *Sunshine,* and the whereabouts of her 40 pounds of gold, has never been solved.

BEAR GREASE

C.O. Rhodes was informed by his wife that she was running desperately short of bear grease for cooking and that if he did not go hunting and bring back a fat bear, she would not be able to bake the bread and pastries that he enjoyed so much. Encouraged by his stomach, C.O. and a friend, Frank Goodpasture, went bear hunting.

C.O. recalled what happened when they spotted a bear digging up an ant pile near a thicket of salmon berries. "We both fired our rifles, but because of the brush and the fact we didn't have a clear shot, we only succeeded in wounding the animal. He disappeared into the thicket.

"Now it is always dangerous to follow a crippled bear into the brush but we were able to climb on top of a windfall and in that manner able to look down and watch the progress of the bear by the motion of the brush as he pushed his way through. After proceeding about a hundred yards he appeared to stop. I told Frank to stay where he was and said that I was going down in the brush to try and roust Mr. Bear.

"I could not find any sign and upon reaching a large stump I climbed as high as I could and commenced to pitching chunks of wood and bark at any likely place in which the bear might be hiding. Sure enough, I scared him out. And what did he do? Ran straight at me. I rapidly climbed to the top of the stump. To my complete surprise I found I had dislodged a yellow jacket's nest but, by then, Frank had gained a position of vantage. He shot the bear. And I was thankful I did not have to make the decision whether to stay where I was and face those vicious little insects, or join the wounded bear on the ground."

DRIVING OUT THE DEVIL

"My parents crossed the Plains by wagon in 18 and 53," related Aeolia Royal. "Father was a religious man, a preacher by vocation, and his fervent purpose in life was to search for and attempt to drive the devil out of the most ungodly of places.

"I suppose that was what brought him to southern Oregon and the settlement on Jackson Creek. It was indeed a wild place, just as any mining camp would be, a strange and volatile mix of the rougher elements of society. Pound for pound there were probably more sinners in that boomtown than anywhere in the land.

"Well do I remember, as a little girl sitting on Father's lap, listening to him tell me how he went about raising money to build his church. He knew the miners were generally in one of two places, either digging for gold or spending it in the saloons.

"My father told me, 'A man so engaged has little time for the Lord but I quickly discovered men will often tolerate, and in some instances even embrace the Almighty, while they are drinking. I would step inside those dens of iniquity and see men gambling, stacks of $20 gold pieces and pokes of gold dust in leather sacks piled high on the table. In such a setting I would begin with a prayer, speaking loudly over the din, and the men, out of respect, would not gamble or drink while I was praying.

"'The saloon keepers learned I was bad for business and whenever I made an appearance in one of their establishments they quickly called for a collection. Most of the men contributed generously and in very short order I had money enough to build my church.'"

REDWOOD CANOE

Indians who lived along the North Pacific were surprised when a storm deposited a giant redwood tree on a beach near their village. They gathered around in awe of such a magnificent sight. The medicine man claimed a great spirit from across the waters had sent the tree. He prayed to the great tree and in time persuaded the tribe to incorporate it into many of their sacred rituals.

One day a visitor came to the village. He said his tribal home lay far to the south, in a land where giant trees grew. He said nothing was sacred about the redwood that had washed up on the beach and announced he was going to carve a canoe from the tree.

The medicine man warned, "The gods will not be pleased. You will be punished."

During the time it took to construct the canoe the stranger won over some members of the tribe. The day the canoe was launched they eagerly took up paddles and the long canoe gracefully rode the waves, responding swiftly to the dictates of the paddlers. They played on the ocean like a water skipper on a quiet pond. Perhaps the medicine man had been wrong.

Late that afternoon disaster struck. A wave picked up the stern and shoved the bow of the canoe underwater. There were sharp cries of panic as Indians were tossed into the water, pulled down and washed out to sea. The giant canoe was battered in the surf and finally rolled ashore. In time it was covered over by the shifting sands.

FAITH

"It seems a part of God's great plan that some people are born to go out and blaze trails and fight the battles of life so that the flag of freedom may be planted in new places. It was that way with my parents," recounted Nancy Osborne.

"My father, Josiah Osborne, had a tendency to tuberculosis and the doctor advised him that the climate in Illinois was not good for his health. At about the same time our local newspaper published several letters exclaiming that there was no place like the far West with its mild weather, abundance of fish and game, wealth of wild berries, and open meadows and towering forests. So on the twelfth day of April, 1845, we loaded up a wagon. How vivid to me yet is the scene that day as we bade adieu to our home and friends; the silent clasping of hands, the well wishes, the tears and the voice of my uncle calling out, 'God bless you on your journey.'

"In our prairie schooner we carried all of our provisions for the next six months: food, clothes, bedding, household equipment, father's chest of tools and a box of books including the histories of Greece and Rome as well as several Bibles. The wagon box was arranged so that the upper part, a corded bedstead, projected over the wheels. Mother could lie down and rest any time that she wished. This she frequently did as the rough jolting of the dead-axle wagon was very tiresome.

"We had two yoke of oxen and one cow. All that we carried constituted our material wealth as we began our long and tiresome journey on the great trail to the West. But whatever we lacked in personal fortune was abundantly replaced by our courage and constant faith that, no matter where we wandered or what ordeals were to befall us, God would be taking care of our needs."

CHRISTMAS MORNING

"I shall do my best to describe Christmas morning when I was a child," said Harriet Adams. "An air of expectancy invaded our household. My older sister was quite active in fostering the Christmas spirit. She read stories to us and I remember my delight when she showed us pictures of that jolly, white-bearded man with a sleigh full of presents pulled by reindeer, and read the words, 'T'was the night before Christmas, and all through the house....'

"One year I questioned how St. Nick could get into our house since it was an impossibility for him to fit through any of our chimneys. I took my concern to Mother. She said that when the chimney was not adequate parents would leave the front door slightly ajar so that St. Nick could push his way inside. This was a most reasonable solution and I was fully satisfied.

"On Christmas Eve our family hiked up the hill and selected a cedar tree. Father chopped it down with his axe and we carried it home. We set it up in the center of the living room and everyone attached small pieces of tin, that would later become candleholders, to the branches. At that point it was time for the little folk to get to bed for under no circumstances could any child be awake when Santa arrived.

"We arose early on Christmas morning but we could not view the tree until after breakfast was eaten. After the meal the children lined up at the door, the youngest in front, and the door was opened and we ran in. The tree was a thing of absolute beauty, the candles all lit, festooned with strings of cranberries and popcorn and gay-colored ribbons. We searched in the branches for gifts and took down our stockings."

WIFE AND MOTHER

Anna Maria Pittman was a 32-year-old spinster. One day she listened to the Reverend Jason Lee speak about the mission he was establishing in the West and she decided to devote her life to missionary work.

In July 1836 Anna Maria boarded a sailing ship in her home state of New York and traveled more than 20,000 miles around Cape Horn to the wilds of the Pacific Northwest. She was taken upriver in an Indian canoe to the small mission established along the Willamette River.

Anna Maria was assigned the tasks of cooking all meals and teaching the Indian children who lived at the mission. The Reverend Jason Lee, mission superintendent, was impressed with Anna Maria's hard work and her fervent devotion to the missionary cause. Within weeks of her arrival he asked for her hand and they were married in a picturesque grove of towering fir trees.

The following spring Jason announced that he needed to make the long overland trip to the East Coast to solicit recruits and financial support. He informed Anna Maria he would return the following year. His departure was difficult because Anna Maria was six months pregnant. The last month of Anna Maria's pregnancy was difficult and when the baby, a boy, was born he lived only two days. Anna Maria faltered, too. Near sunrise on June 26, 1838 she opened her eyes and murmured, "I am going to my rest." And she died.

The mother and her infant son were laid together in the same grove of fir trees where Anna Maria had so recently been married. Two months later a messenger caught up with Jason at Westport, Missouri and delivered the tragic news to him.

HOMESICK

"The first school I ever attended was in Oregon City shortly after we crossed the Plains. That was in 18 and 46," related Marianne Hunsaker.

"My father helped put up the log building for the school. The fireplace was of rock and the chimney of sticks plastered over with clay. The floors were heavy timbers, roughly dressed, and our benches were slabs with pegs driven into them for legs. I walked to school barefooted until Father could obtain some tanned leather and make shoes.

"After several years Father built a sawmill on the north side of the Columbia River. By that time the Sisters of Notre Dame had started a school and Father arranged for me to board with them and attend school there. After Father, Mother and the two babies departed I became so terribly lonely for them that I cried myself to sleep nearly every night. One of the older girls at the school tried to comfort me, saying that most all the children at the school were orphans.

"'What are orphans?' I asked between sobs.

"'They are children who are left behind. Either their folks have gone to the gold fields in California or they are dead.'

"This revelation made me so panic-stricken that I nearly fainted. I thought I should never see my family again. It was not until November of that year that Father sold his mill and he and Mother and the two little ones returned to Oregon City. Days after their arrival my brother Lycurgus was born. And again, much to my relief, we began living together as a family."

HIGH SEA MARRIAGE

"Father was a strict disciplinarian and would not allow me or my sisters to keep company with young men until we reached the ripe old age of 18," recalled Mrs. Kamm. "However, I did receive several proposals of marriage and referred each of the young men to Father. He discouraged them quite effectively. But then I met Jacob Kamm and I knew he was the man I would marry."

"I decided not to take a chance on sending Jacob to see Father, but I myself went to the Fraser River in Canada where Father was operating a boat during the gold excitement that was happening there. I broke the news of my proposed engagement and he took it pretty well.

"Jacob joined me and though we planned to marry immediately we found the laws of British Columbia even more strict than those of the United States. Our only alternative seemed to be to marry in neutral waters. On September 13, 1859, we took a minister with us and boarded a boat. Jacob and I were married on the high seas. The miners aboard, who were returning from the gold diggings in British Columbia, witnessed the ceremony and cheered us heartily.

"I have lived a long life. I have seen almost unbelievable changes in my 87 years. The young people of the present generation think of the days when I was a girl as a time of hardship and hard work. It is true that in those days everyone worked, but it is also true that we managed to have mighty pleasant times, too. We enjoyed our trips by canoe or horseback. We had more time to be friendly and, it seems to me, more disposition to be helpful and of service to others than young people seem to have today."

MOTORCYCLE RACER

"My son Otto came down with typhoid fever. He was terribly sick and at one point I made the mistake of telling him that if he would hurry and get well he could have one of those new-fangled motorcycles. He was crazy for having a motorcycle," recalled Mrs. Walker.

Otto was sick for thirteen weeks and then he crawled out of bed, went downtown and bought a motorcycle. He began riding every day and after regaining his strength he entered several amateur races. He did so well that in 1915 the Harley-Davidson Motor Company signed him to race on their team. They gave him $200 a month, paid his expenses and allowed him to keep the prize money. The first year he pocketed $6,700.

Otto claimed his first world record in a 300-mile race in which he averaged a trifle better than 69 miles per hour. He went on to hold, at one time or another, every world's record from one to 300 miles. But along with the records came accidents. In the 50-mile National Championship, two riders went down in front of him and rather than ride over them Otto steered straight for a heavy guardrail and the momentum threw him high into the air. In a letter to his mother Otto wrote, "Both shoulders were dislocated, as well as both knees. I broke my thumb in three places and cut my lip, requiring 17 stitches. Aside from that, I came out pretty well."

Mrs. Walker recalled, "Otto raced competitively for 11 years. His worst wreck was when he was in a coma for 16 hours. An overzealous newspaperman, who did not expect him to live, wrote his obituary. After Otto came awake and read that I think it dawned on him just how precious life was. He sold his motorcycle. That was the happiest day of my life."

MOUNTAIN FEVER

"We started for Oregon in 1852. That was a bad year for disease and many in our wagon train suffered dreadfully and died. My husband and I stayed relatively healthy until we crossed over the Blue Mountains, then we both came down with mountain fever," related Mrs. Willis Boatman.

"After several days my health began to improve slightly but my husband was so bad off he never expected to get up again. At one point he told me that when he died I was to sell the wagon and remaining team and try to arrange passage back to the States and my people.

"Over the course of a week his health slowly began to improve. We arranged passage downriver on a scow to Portland. There were only about twenty houses total in the settlement but we were able to find shelter, meager as it was, in a shed that was open to the weather. That night we made our bed on the dirt floor and felt lucky because this was the first roof we had been under for seven long months. Lying there we began to realize our situation. Here we were at journey's end, three thousand miles from our relatives, in poor health, without money and little more than a simple roof over our heads. There was not much sleep that night.

"The following day my husband managed to get some work cutting firewood, but soon was taken down with the chills and fever. I, too, became sick and we had to call in a doctor who could do very little for us except present us with a bill, which only added to our misery.

"I was able to overcome my infirmity and go to work but it was fully six weeks before the fever and shakes subsided in my husband. But finally there came the time when we were healthy once again and were able to begin forging our new life."

THE DREAM

"My husband and I had five children and a pocketful of dreams," recalled Mrs. McMahon. "We decided to file on a homestead and, with a lot of hard work, we set out to make those dreams come true."

Four years after filing on the homestead in southern Colorado the dream turned into a nightmare. Mr. McMahon became so sick he could not get out of bed and within a few months he was dead.

Mrs. McMahon vowed to keep the homestead and raise her children there. They planted a crop of corn and it grew tall and held the promise of a wonderful yield. But a week before harvest one of the kids came running into the house, calling out, "Momma, there's a strange cloud in the sky. Have a look an' see."

The cloud descended from the blue sky and suddenly grasshoppers were everywhere, flying around, making it hard to breathe, piling up on the ground until they were ankle deep. The family took refuge in the root cellar while the grasshoppers marched on the cornfield like an invading army. Two days later, when the family emerged from the root cellar, it appeared the corn crop had been cut with a hand scythe.

That fall the rains never came to dampen the soil. Instead, the wind began to blow and it carried away the topsoil. The river was reduced to a trickle, and then it dried up and quit running.

Mrs. McMahon knew that all her dreams were dead. She gathered her children and hand in hand they hiked up the road to the top of the hill. Here they paused and looked back. Tears flowed freely. And then they continued walking to town, where Mrs. McMahon found work—cleaning houses for wealthy people.

TRICK RIDER

Tad Barnes was the youngest of 24 children. She rose from the humblest of beginnings to become the greatest female trick rider of all time.

Her first ride on a wild bronc occurred when she was 8 years old. She lasted only a couple jumps and was thrown to the ground. But she never forgot the thrill of that ride. At the age of 14 she began competing in relay horse races and women's steer riding contests. She joined a wild west show touring the country and before long Tad was the star of the show, earning more than $10,000 a year.

Eight times in a row Tad won the World's Trick Riding Championship at Madison Square Garden in New York City. She toured Europe, performing trick riding as well as bronc riding and relay racing. But the good times ended at the Chicago World's Fair in 1933. Tad was performing a trick where she rolled under the belly of her horse as it raced full speed across the arena. This time she dropped too low and the horse's hoof struck her left arm, shattering the bone. Doctors said the arm would most certainly have to be amputated and Tad would never be able to compete again.

Tad proved the doctors wrong. She endured several operations and wore a cast for three years, but she never quit performing and the crowds always cheered her unwavering determination.

Tad competed at the 1958 Brussels World's Fair and when she came home she made one last exhibition at Huntsville, Texas. It was there that she declared she was retiring. "I could keep going," she said, "but my horse is 25 years old and you know, I just don't feel like breaking in another horse."

POWER TO PREACH

"The country was in the middle of the Great Depression but my husband had a job and my babies and I were well provided for," stated Mrs. Coons. "And then one day, out of the blue, my husband had a religious conversion. He claimed that God had spoken to him. After that nothing was ever the same."

Mr. Coons quit his job, bought a truck and built a house on the back. He covered every inch of the surface of the house with words, verses, scriptures and slogans: "Jesus Saves" and "Ye Must Be Born Again". When he was finished Mr. Coons moved his wife and children into the house on wheels and they went on the road.

They stopped at every town and Mr. Coons preached fire and brimstone; promising good folks eternal salvation in heaven and claiming that sinners were doomed to the devil's fire. Sometimes the spirit dwelled in him and he was able to lay his hand on people and actually heal their physical ailments. When miracles like this occurred Mr. Coons would become obsessed with his powers and so excited he would be unable to sleep for several days.

Near the end of each service Mrs. Coons walked among the crowd and asked for donations. But money was hard to come by and the only thing that kept the family on the road was the generosity of the farmers who donated a few gallons of gas, eggs, milk, peas, potatoes and sometimes a rump roast or a side of bacon.

The depression worsened and the months of living hand-to-mouth took a toll on Mr. Coons. He gradually lost his ability to heal and then to preach. But through those desperate times he never once lost his faith.

FEATHERS

"My earliest memories are of the Indians and the occasional white man who came to my father's trading post," related Louisa Sinclair. "In those days there was very little actual currency on the North Pacific coast and as a result, supplies were exchanged according to a barter system. Feathers were in strong demand for filling such important items as pillows and bed ticks. Father bought all he could. As a result the Indians killed ducks as much for their feathers as for food.

"The feathers were tied together into a bale and the exchange was made according to how many pounds the bale weighed. One time Father insisted on inspecting a bale that a local Indian brought to the trading post. His suspicion proved accurate as less than half of the bale was feathers and the remainder, tucked out of sight, was composed of twigs and dirt clods.

"This particular Indian was infuriated that his deception had been discovered and with wild gestures and in a loud, angry voice he raved that Father did not trust him. He claimed that someone had slipped the foreign substances into the bale to make him look bad and in a final demonstration of his outrage he fiercely kicked the open bale. Feathers flew everywhere. They flew up to the ceiling, rolling along like a cloud across the room and then slowly, very slowly, they began to settle. Feathers covered everything.

"The Indian insisted he be paid for the amount of the bale that had been feathers and Father agreed on the condition they be gathered up into a bale. This proved too much of a job for the Indian and he stormed away. A number of weeks passed before we, at long last, swept up the last feather."

PROVING UP

"The government opened up homestead ground in the Fort Rock Valley of Oregon. Henry, my husband, and I talked it over and decided to give it a try," recalled Loie Horning. "We moved onto 320 acres of desert ground.

"We built our house board-and-batten style with nothing but tar paper on the inside. It was cold enough that in the mornings the tack heads would be white with frost. The soil was wonderful and would grow almost anything if it had water. I saved our wash water for the garden and we tried to grow vegetables but the frost, which could come most any month of the year, got more of the vegetables than we ever did.

"Henry and I were blessed with two children, Johnie and Elva. In 1917 little Johnie took sick with scarlet fever and we were quarantined for four weeks. After that he came down with pneumonia. He got over it but Henry caught the bug and ten days later he died.

"The children and I had no money and no place to go. We stayed on and proved up on the homestead in five years. To earn a little extra money I became the postmaster at Wastina. My pay, based on the number of stamp cancellations I made on outgoing mail, was a grand total of $17 the first three months I worked.

"Some of the women in the neighborhood thought the desert a dreadful place to live but after we left there I was lonesome for it. Even now I sometimes shut my eyes and I can still hear the way the coyotes serenaded us and in my mind I go over the scenes of the fun things we used to do."

Loie and the children moved from the homestead in the late 1920s. They moved to Michigan and Loie passed away in 1985, at the age of 103.

HOMESTEADING SISTERS

Sisters Anna and Millie Steinhoff were living in Portland, Oregon when word circulated that free homestead land was available east of the Cascade Mountains. In the fall of 1910 they filed on adjoining 160-acre parcels and arranged to have a home constructed that straddled their allotments.

Reaching their new home proved to be an ordeal. The sisters took the train to the end of the line and then, for the next forty-one hours, they rode a pitching, swaying stage. The driver stopped in the middle of a sagebrush sea and from here the two sisters had to hike more than two miles to their homesteads. Anna noted in her diary they carried "grips with our clothes, a quilt, one length of stove pipe and a broom. Upon our arrival we found that although a shack had been built for us it had absolutely nothing in it."

For the first several months the sisters had to hike a mile to the nearest neighbor, pump water from their well and carry it home in a washtub. But they managed to hand-dig their own well and were able to pump water to the surface. They grubbed out the sagebrush, planted grain and lived off the land as much as they could. They hunted rabbits, ducks, geese and swans.

Most of those who homesteaded were either single men or married couples and families. Single women homesteaders were few and far between and as a result the Steinhoff sisters attracted a great deal of attention. Anna made the following notation in her diary: "This afternoon one of the bachelor neighbors came for a visit. He brought me a rabbit. We talked of very sensible subjects until dusk and then his conversation suddenly drifted to matrimony. I was honored with his proposal but I promptly sent him on his way with my refusal."

Rick Steber's Tales of the Wild West series feature illustrations by Don Gray. The AudioBooks are narrated by Dallas McKennon. Current titles in the series include:

Other books written by Rick Steber—

www.ricksteber.com

Bonanza Publishing
Box 204
Prineville, Oregon 97754